GOOD D🐾G

8

PUPPY LUCK

by Cam
Higgins

illustrated by
Ariel Landy

LITTLE SIMON

New York London Toronto Sydney New Delhi

LITTLE SIMON
An imprint of Simon & Schuster Children's Publishing Division
1230 Avenue of the Americas, New York, New York 10020
First Little Simon paperback edition May 2022
Copyright © 2022 by Simon & Schuster, Inc.
Also available in a Little Simon hardcover edition.
All rights reserved, including the right of reproduction in whole or in part in any form. LITTLE SIMON is a registered trademark of Simon & Schuster, Inc., and associated colophon is a trademark of Simon & Schuster, Inc.
For information about special discounts for bulk purchases, please contact Simon & Schuster Special Sales at 1-866-506-1949 or business@simonandschuster.com.
The Simon & Schuster Speakers Bureau can bring authors to your live event. For more information or to book an event contact the Simon & Schuster Speakers Bureau at 1-866-248-3049 or visit our website at www.simonspeakers.com.
Designed by Leslie Mechanic
Manufactured in the United States of America 0422 MTN
10 9 8 7 6 5 4 3 2 1
Library of Congress Cataloging-in-Publication Data
Names: Higgins, Cam, author. | Landy, Ariel, illustrator.
Title: Puppy luck / by Cam Higgins ; illustrated by Ariel Landy.
Description: First Little Simon edition. | New York : Little Simon, 2022. | Series: Good dog ; #8 | Audience: Ages 5–9. | Summary: After a bout of bad luck, Bo and his friends search for a way to bring back his puppy luck.
Identifiers: LCCN 2021054003 (print) | LCCN 2021054004 (ebook) | ISBN 9781665905916 (paperback) | ISBN 9781665905923 (hardcover) | ISBN 9781665905930 (ebook) | Subjects: CYAC: Dogs—Fiction. | Animals—Infancy—Fiction. | Luck—Fiction. | Farm life—Fiction. | Classification: LCC PZ7.1.H54497 Pu 2022 (print) | LCC PZ7.1.H54497 (ebook) | DDC [E]—dc23
LC record available at https://lccn.loc.gov/2021054003

CONTENTS

New Color, New Coop?

The sun was shining brightly in the sky. Glimmers of golden light fell across the fields and trees. What a beautiful day!

And it was an exciting day too. I was so happy for Clucks, Rufus, and all the chicks. Their coop was getting a brand-new paint job!

Jennica and Darnell, my human parents, had made the design, and Imani and Wyatt, my human sister and brother, were going to paint. They had all the tools they needed—paint, brushes, rollers, and pans. Everything was lined up on a large piece of tarp.

"We're going to paint the coop red—
to match the barn," Jennica explained
to the kids. "And we'll give it a nice
white trim, too."

All the animals watched as Darnell
brushed the first stroke of bright red
paint over the wood panel. Clucks
pecked at the ground excitedly.

"Oooh, I can't wait to see what our new home looks like!" she cried. "Rufus, aren't you thrilled too?"

Rufus strutted past, a bored look on his face.

"Sure, sure, although it isn't exactly a new coop," he crowed. He clearly was not anywhere near as amused as Clucks was.

"Yes, but the new red color will make it *feel* like new!" she replied.

"You're right. The red color *is* very nice," Zonks chimed in. "But I would have gone with a bright pink color. You know, like the color of—*ahem*—a pig!"

"Naaah, not pink!" Comet neighed. "Turquoise and orange zigzags are more like me! That would have been so cool."

I woofed out a laugh. Turquoise and orange zigzags would have looked pretty wild, all right.

"Bo, what do you—" Zonks started to ask, right as I spotted something out of the corner of my eye.

It was something small and gray and fluffy. And something that made me freeze in place and think, *Oh, SQUIRREL!*

I stared at the squirrel, and the squirrel stared at me. Moments passed. My ears perked up. My tail swished.

The squirrel stood up. And then he bolted.

The squirrel darted across the field and ran up a tree, right above the chicken coop.

I chased him at top speed. But that probably wasn't the best idea. Because as I rushed by, I knocked  over a can of white paint! The fresh paint splashed all over Wyatt's and Imani's clothes before they could get out of the way.

"Awww, Bo! Come back here!" Imani shouted. "You're making a total mess!"

10

A Painty, Soapy Mess

Oopsie daisy! Did I really do that?

I knew Imani wasn't happy, but I really couldn't help it! Dogs *must* chase squirrels. It's just a fact. Luckily, Wyatt was giggling when I ran back. At least *one* human thought it was funny.

Right then, Jennica reached for me.

But I zipped past her, my eyes still focused on my target.

"Hey, Bo! Calm down! Stay!" Darnell called.

The squirrel snatched an acorn from the branch he was sitting on. Then he hopped from the tree to the roof of the coop.

The squirrel stared down at me as he nibbled noisily on his acorn.

I jumped and pawed toward him as hard as I could, but I wasn't tall enough. I scrambled along to the other side. No matter what I did, I couldn't get to him.

I watched as the squirrel finished eating his acorn, leaped off the roof, and bounded toward the forest.

I started after him, ready to pounce. But then I felt a tug on my collar.

"Oh, no you don't!" Jennica said, sweeping me up. "You aren't going anywhere but the bath." Then she turned to Wyatt and Imani. "After you get changed out of those paint-covered clothes, give this naughty boy a bath."

That's when I snapped out of it and saw what I'd done. A trail of white paw prints covered the side of Clucks and Rufus's newly painted coop.

"Please keep Bo away until we're all done painting," Jennica said, leaning over to give me a kiss.

I was glad that she didn't seem too mad. But I knew I had made a big, messy mistake.

Wyatt clipped my leash to my collar and led me inside. "Come on, boy."

When we got to the bathroom, Imani and Wyatt ran a nice hot bath with lots of bubbles. They took turns rubbing the shampoo into my fur. I tried my best to stay still.

But I kept hearing a strange buzzing
in my ear, and it was growing louder
and louder. What could it possibly be?

Suddenly, something tiny and yellow and black flitted in front of my eyes . . . and landed on my nose! It was a bumblebee! *Oh, no!*

When I was a pup,
I had a very scary
meeting with a wasp.
They have a sharp and
pointy stinger that hurts
a lot. And so do bees!

I barked loudly and leaped out of
the tub. My face was covered in soap.
But I knew the bumblebee was still on
my nose. I ran out of the bathroom,
shaking my head to get the bee off.

"Hey, Bo!" Wyatt called. "Stop, hang on! You're getting everything wet!"

He bent down and covered me with a towel. But there was no time to wait. I had to get out of there as fast as I could.

Stung!

I dashed down the stairs and headed for my doggy door. This bee needed to be out of our house right away! But rushing was probably another bad idea. I missed the last step of the front porch . . . and landed on the ground with a loud THUD.

All of a sudden I couldn't see a thing.

Did someone turn the lights off?

I realized the towel was over my face. So I shook my body to get it off, when I heard the buzzing again. Only now it sounded angry!

The bumblebee was still circling me, and it was getting louder.

Before I could run, it zoomed

toward me and stuck its stinger right in my nose.

OUCH!

I rolled over and held my nose. At first, I was in shock. But then the pain set in.

My nose was throbbing and hurt so much.

First the squirrel, then the paint, and now this bee? I couldn't believe it. What bad luck! Could things get any worse?

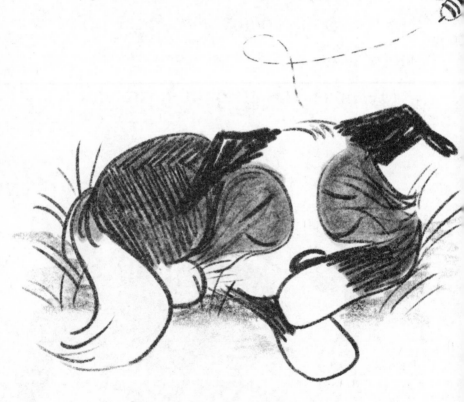

And that's when I heard my answer.

ZAP! I jumped as a giant clap of thunder crashed somewhere in the distance. And just like that, rain started pouring down.

The front door swung open, and
a very worried-looking Imani and
Wyatt rushed outside.

I let out a sneeze, which made my
nose hurt even more.

"Oh, no! Come on, Bo, let's get you inside," Imani said, picking me up. I let out a small whimper as she carried me into the house.

She and Wyatt then brought me back upstairs to the bathroom and ran another hot bath. Imani gently placed me inside, and they washed away all the mud.

My nose still hurt. But the warm water did calm me down.

After I was finally clean and dry, Imani took a look at my face.

"We'd better get some baking soda to take care of that nasty bee sting," she said.

So Wyatt mixed some baking soda and water into a paste and tenderly applied it to my nose.

I sniffed and barked a thank-you.

"Aw, Bo, sorry about your nose," Imani said. "How about a treat to help you feel better?"

I perked up a little and followed her down to the kitchen.

I waited, happily wagging my tail. But then another bad thing happened.

The thunderstorm was still brewing outside, and it seemed to be getting worse. Suddenly, a loud clap of thunder raised the hair on my back. I skittered out of the kitchen as fast as I could and dove under the couch.

Yikes, that was scary!

"Oh, Bo!" Imani called, hurrying out to follow me. She bent down in front of the couch to look at me. "Come on out, boy. It's okay."

"Yeah, come on, Bo," Wyatt called. "The loud thunder can't hurt you."

But I wasn't going to budge. Nothing my humans said was going to get me out from under the couch tonight.

More
Bad Luck!

My humans will probably never understand, but the space underneath the couch is pretty cozy. And it's the perfect place for a puppy nap!

But soon I woke up because my stomach started to grumble.

So I slid out from under the couch, stood up, and stretched my body.

The rain had stopped, and the sun was shining. The storm clouds were finally gone.

Outside I saw that Jennica and Darnell had spread a tarp over the top of the chicken coop to keep it dry. I decided it was safe to take a closer look. But when I drew near, I could see the big white paw prints on the side.

And that's when Clucks walked over.

"Naughty Bo!" she clucked. "Look what you did to our beautiful coop!"

"Oh, Clucks," I woofed. "I'm really sorry! I didn't mean to."

I felt terrible. Turns out, a good nap doesn't fix everything.

As I left the chicken coop, I bumped into my barnyard buddies, Comet and Zonks. From the worried looks on their faces, I knew they knew. Word travels fast around this farm.

"Hey, Bo, don't look so sad," Comet neighed. "It wasn't your fault. Accidents happen all the time!"

"Yeah, you didn't mean any trouble," Zonks oinked. "And I have just the thing to make you smile!"

I looked down and shook my head. I wasn't sure anything could make me feel better.

"A visit from a best bud! Look!" Zonks cried, pointing toward the woods with his snout.

And sure enough, Scrapper, my
best dog pal, was coming over.

Scrapper quickly ran to where
Comet, Zonks, and I stood.

"Hey, guys! Did you see that amazing light show in the sky?" he barked excitedly. "It was awesome!" Then Scrapper paused and took a long look at me. "Wait a minute. What's wrong with you, Bo?"

Oh gosh, where should I begin? I wondered.

First I told him about the squirrel. I knew that Scrapper would understand. Dogs know that dogs need to chase squirrels. But that led to paint, paw prints, a bath . . . and then a bee!

I stopped to take a breath. Scrapper was still listening intently.

Thinking about everything made me feel bad all over again. Bad luck was on my tail and wasn't going to let go.

"Ohhh, a thunderstorm!" cried Scrapper. "So that's what the cool light show was!"

I couldn't believe that Scrapper
thought the loud thunder was cool. I
guess not all dogs are the same, huh?

"I know exactly what you need,
Bo!" Scrapper barked. "It'll help bring
back your puppy luck!"

A Puppy
Luck Charm

I looked up at Scrapper with a twinkle in my eye. I've been a dog my whole life, but I had no idea my puppy luck was missing! As usual, I was glad that Scrapper knew things I didn't.

"Really? What's that?" I asked.

"A trusty puppy luck charm, of course!" Scrapper replied proudly.

"Ummm, what's a puppy luck charm?" I asked.

"Well, it's something you carry around with you to keep the stormy bad-luck clouds away," he explained.

"What does it have to be?" I asked, confused.

Was he talking about a dog bone or a sock or a stick? Those were things I played with all the time. But I didn't think they were lucky.

"Well, for example, maybe you could find a lucky acorn," Scrapper suggested.

"Hmmm, but acorns are squirrel food," I said, frowning. "And I don't think squirrels bring me good puppy luck."

"Oh, that's a good point," Scrapper said. Then he got up and started to look around.

I wanted to help, but I had no idea what he was looking for.

"That's it! I got it!" he cried. "Comet, what are those, um, sneakers you wear on your hooves?"

"You mean my *horseshoes*?" Comet whinnied, lifting a hoof to show us one of the metal shoes.

"Yeah, that's it! Horseshoes are good luck!" Scrapper said. "And so are those white cubes humans play games with!"

"Sugar cubes?" Comet asked.

"No, you can't eat these. I mean the ones with spots on them."

"Oh, dice," Zonks said helpfully.

60

I had no idea
how a pig knew
what dice were. But
that made me smile
big. Zonks always
had an answer for
everything.

"Yep. Those can bring good puppy luck. And so can four-leaf clovers," Scrapper said.

And that's when Zonks perked up.

"Oooh, I know where we can find a four-leaf clover!" he oinked. "In the meadow near the forest!"

"Well, off to the meadow we go!"
Scrapper barked. "It's time to help Bo
find his puppy luck again!"

On the Hunt

The sweet scent of rain and grass filled the meadow. Sunshine peeked out from the clouds and warmed my back.

The four of us decided to split up to search for a lucky four-leaf clover. Zonks warned us that it wouldn't be easy to find, and we didn't have much time before the sun would set.

Scrapper and I headed to a patch next to the forest, while Zonks and Comet set off for a clover patch in the other direction.

We kept our eyes glued to the ground, searching for the special clover that would bring me good luck.

But after digging and digging, none of us could find one.

I watched as Zonks spotted a butterfly and took off after it. Zonks was a great friend. But even pigs get distracted by butterflies sometimes.

The sun was now lower in the sky, and I was starting to get nervous. What if we never found one?

I knew I needed to shake it off and stay focused. It was too early to give up, especially with my friends helping.

Suddenly I heard a soft buzzing noise. It was a bee! Flying around Scrapper!

I couldn't let my best friend get stung. I had to save him!

My heart sped up as I raced over to Scrapper, who was perched on a fallen tree log. All I needed to do was give him a gentle push to get him out of the bee's path.

Except I think that little push was
more like a hard shove. Scrapper fell
off the log, landed on his side, and let
out a yelp.

Comet and Zonks raced over as soon as they heard Scrapper's cry.

I felt terrible. I was trying to help my friend, but instead I hurt him. I think Scrapper was, luckily, more shocked than hurt. But that's when I knew it.

Looking for this puppy luck charm wasn't going to help me.

I was officially bad luck for everyone. So the best thing I could do was to stay away from my friends.

A Sky
Full of Color

As I walked along, I spotted a set of familiar tracks with a bunch of acorns and decided to follow it. Squirrels may not be good news for me, but I just couldn't help it.

I followed the small prints all the way to the swimming hole. I watched as the water glimmered before me.

I trotted to the edge of the trees and stopped. There was a strange light reflecting off the surface of the water. What could that be?

I hopped up and down to try to get a better look, but I was too small to see.

As I paced back and forth, my
friends caught up to me.

"There you are, Bo!" Scrapper cried.
"We've been looking for you!"

"Aw, I'm sorry, Scrapper," I said quietly. "I didn't mean to make you fall."

I looked down, embarrassed. No amount of puppy luck was going to fix this.

"Don't worry about it, Bo!" Scrapper yipped. "I actually need to thank you! Comet told me there was a bee."

"Yeah, you're a good friend," Comet added. "And I think your puppy luck might be close. Look up there!" She held her head toward the sky.

I hopped up but still couldn't see a thing.

"Here, Bo. Climb up here," Comet said. She pointed her nose at a big rock, then gave me a gentle nudge toward it.

Now I could see it! The sky was full of color. It was a dazzling burst of red, orange, yellow, green, and blue. I had never seen anything like it before.

"Wow! What *is* that?" I asked.

"A rainbow, of course!" Zonks said matter-of-factly. "They're super hard to find. But after a storm, if you're very lucky, a rainbow will appear!"

I looked over at Zonks in awe. He really was the smartest pig I knew.

"Hey, Bo! You know what that means?" Zonks oinked. "Your puppy luck is close by!"

Scrapper and I barked in excitement

while Comet neighed happily.

My puppy luck charm had to be somewhere over that beautiful rainbow, and I couldn't wait to find it.

A Double Surprise

We made our way through the woods back to the meadow. Once we were out in the open field and away from the canopy of tree branches, we could see how dazzling the sky was.

There wasn't just one rainbow— there were two! It was a *double* rainbow!

"Wow, I couldn't see the second rainbow in the woods!" Zonks said excitedly.

"Me neither. It's so beautiful!" Scrapper barked.

I jumped up and twirled around. This magical double rainbow had to be a sign!

The bubbly feeling I get in my tummy whenever I know something good is about to happen filled me up. Like whenever I find a giant mud puddle to jump in, or when my human family opens my special treat cabinet.

And I knew then—the four-leaf
clover I was searching for had to be
at the end of those double rainbows!
I barked with joy and ran through the
field toward them.

But when I reached the spot where the two rainbows met, I stopped short and looked around. Suddenly all the beautiful colors had faded, and I couldn't see anything. Did I somehow chase the rainbows away?

My tail drooped, and my heart sank. I was so confused.

But in the distance I heard my friends cheering. And I knew I couldn't give up yet.

So I put my nose to the grass and started sniffing. I walked in circles until the sweet perfume of flowers drifted to my nose. I picked up my head to get a better look.

And, oh my gosh, there it was.

Right in the middle of a patch of flowers, I spied the perfect four-leaf clover!

9

Chasing Rainbows

Scrapper and Comet were the first to reach me. Zonks followed close behind them.

When they noticed the velvety-soft green four-leaf clover, all three of my friends began to cheer.

"Hooray, Bo!" Comet whinnied. "You found it!"

Zonks rolled merrily in the grass, oinking with joy.

Scrapper leaned close to me and said, "See, buddy, you aren't bad luck at all! Between the clover and the rainbows, you've got double the good luck!"

"What are you going to do with the four-leaf clover now?" Zonks asked.

I smiled a doggy smile. I knew exactly what I wanted to do with it.

"Come on!" I called.

I bounded off back to the farm with my friends in tow.

When we arrived at the barnyard, my human family was back at work, putting the finishing touches on the chicken coop.

Clucks, Rufus, and the chicks were standing a little way back, watching Jennica, Darnell, Imani, and Wyatt paint.

But I didn't hang back. I ran right up to them with the four-leaf clover in my mouth. Then I dropped it on the ground and barked loudly to get their attention. Wyatt and Imani leaped up and came over to me first. Wyatt scratched my head while Imani picked up the clover.

"Look, Mom! Bo found something—it's a four-leaf clover!" Imani said excitedly.

Jennica came over to see.

"Good boy, Bo! Four-leaf clovers are very rare!" she cried.

That's when Darnell glanced up at the wall above the door of the chicken coop.

There was a blank space, perfect for adding a nice decoration.

"I have an idea!" he said. "How about we frame Bo's four-leaf clover and hang it on top of the chicken coop?"

"Yes! That sounds awesome!" Wyatt and Imani exclaimed.

I wagged my tail happily in response. Things were finally starting to get better!

10

A
Happy End

As I was turning around to head inside the house, Clucks and Rufus strutted over to me.

Clucks pecked at the ground. I held my breath. Was the clover a bad idea? Did she not like it?

But luckily Clucks looked up at me with a big smile.

"Bo, thank you so much for the clover. We love it," Clucks said. "I'm sorry if I hurt your feelings earlier."

I wagged my tail and smiled back at her. I was glad that she liked it.

"We chickens have been so excited for our new coop," she continued. "So I was just surprised when everything didn't go exactly as planned."

"I know, and I'm sorry about that,"
I replied. "But I'm so glad you like my
present."

Clucks and Rufus nodded and
walked off as Scrapper came over.

"Hey, Bo! Are you sure you want
to give away your puppy luck?" he
asked. "Finding a lucky four-leaf
clover doesn't happen often!"

I nodded and let out a happy bark.

"Scrapper, I don't think a puppy luck charm is what makes you feel lucky," I said. "But I think I have figured how to keep my puppy luck with me!"

"Really?" Scrapper piped up. "How?"

"It's been inside me this whole time!" I cried. "I just needed to believe in myself, look for the rainbows, and follow my heart!"

Scrapper let out another excited bark.

"It's thanks to you, Zonks, and Comet," I added. "You showed me that I wasn't a bad luck magnet after all."

Some pups might go chasing after luck, like I tried to chase the rainbow. But my friends reminded me that I just had to slow down. That's when I realized my puppy luck was right in front of me the whole time.

After a long day, it was time for Scrapper to go. The sun was setting, and he needed to get back to his own human family.

Then I said good-bye to Zonks and Comet. As I started back toward the house, Imani's voice rang out.

"Hey, Bo! We have a special project, and we need all hands and paws on deck!"

The next morning I woke up with a big puppy stretch. Yesterday, before the sun went to bed, Wyatt and Imani put another coat of paint on the chicken coop. And guess what—I got to help! And this time I was super careful not to run in any paint.

I couldn't wait to see how the coop would look now. I even had a dream about how exciting it would be to see it.

"Good morning!" I called to the
chicks.

I ran all around the chicken coop,
barking with happiness. It looked
even better than it did in my dream!

The four-leaf clover hung proudly above the door.

From now on, the coop would remind me that even on the stormiest day, there was always a rainbow waiting on the other side.

But like always, that's when something familiar caught my eye. Something small and gray and fluffy.

Dogs have a good sense of smell.

So I knew right away that the same squirrel was back. And he was still fast.

I watched as he scurried away with as many acorns as he could carry.

I might have missed him this time. But that was okay.

My puppy luck was back. And I had a good, tingly feeling we were going to have a beautiful, blue-skies day. But if it turned out that another storm was on the way, I wouldn't mind that either. Because if my puppy luck ever goes missing again, I now know exactly where to look.

Here's a peek at Bo's next big adventure!

GOOD D🐾G

9

Sweater Weather

The sun glimmered through the clouds as I raced around the barn. There was a fresh, crisp scent in the air. And all the trees were bursting with color.

Wyatt and Imani, my human brother and sister, were busy sweeping the

An excerpt from *Sweater Weather*

leaves. I raced toward them as fast as I could to get a better look. But I got a little too excited and tumbled right into the pile!

Oops! Golden-yellow leaves flew everywhere.

As I ran around in happy circles, the leaves made a loud crunching noise. And the brown ones were the crunchiest.

"Hey, Zonks!" I said in greeting as I ran over to the pen. "Look at these colorful leaves! I wonder why they change."

"That's because fall is here! The

leaves always change when the wind gets cooler," Zonks explained. "It just makes sense, like pigs and mud."

Zonks was right. Some things just made sense. And that's all that mattered.

When I ran back to where Imani and Wyatt were, they were now starting on a new pile.

I was so tempted to jump back in. But then I heard Jennica, my human mom, call my name.